Brampton Stories 1

Carlos R. Medina

Tellwell Talent
www.tellwell.ca

ISBN
978-1-77370-584-2 (Paperback)

Brampton Stories 1

Carlos R. Medina

To my wife and son, Maria Veronica and Theo—
my eloquent interlocutors—
without whom I would merely be soliloquizing.

To my colleagues and students
at the MCS LINC Program, Brampton (Ontario)—
my fellow story-tellers—
as we carpool on our short commute that we call life.

Acknowledgements

Several persons helped me write these five short short stories. Some did not know they were helping me then; others did. Their names are listed alphabetically as follows.

Motivation came from such authors as:

Jack M. Bickham. (1993). *Scene & Structure*. Cincinnati: Writer's Digest Books.

James Scott Bell. (2012). *Revision and Self-Editing for Publication, 2*nd *ed.* Cincinnati: Writer's Digest Books.

Margaret Lucke. (1998). *Schaum's Quick Guide to Writing Great Short Stories*. New York: McGraw-Hill.

Nancy Kress. (2011). *Beginnings, Middles, & Ends.* Cincinnati: Writer's Digest Books.

Orson Scott Card. (2010). *Characters & Viewpoint.* Cincinnati: Writer's Digest Books.

Paul Negri, ed. (2005). *Great Short Short Stories. Quick Reads by Great Writers.* New York: Dover Publications.

Ron Rozelle. (2005). *Description & Setting.* Cincinnati: Writer's Digest Books.

Evaluation and feedback came from instructors and student services staff of Stratford Institute of Creative Writing: Lesley Renaud, Mildred Rainey, Kyle Carney, and Melissa Christopher. Brampton novelist Kenneth Puddicombe (*Racing with the Rain,* 2012 / *Junta,* 2014) reviewed these five short short stories comprehensively. He then collegially advised, "Take my comments with a grain of salt. These are *your* stories; only *you* can decide *your* stories."

Indeed, an analysis of the stories in Paul Negri's *Great Short Short Stories* demonstrates Kenneth Puddicombe's point. Each of those thirty stories is unique. The thirty authors used writing tools—character development, conflict, point of view, drama, narration, resolution, etc.—in different ways. They must have experienced that no one tool is intrinsically "better" than another. While such tools are "objective" in the sense that there is a consensus about them, writing fiction is indeed a solitary art—as Orson Scott Card observed.

I credit the aforementioned authors, instructors, and staff for what they taught me. Whether or not I understood what they taught is— needless to say—arguable.

Carlos R. Medina
Brampton, Ontario
Spring 2018

Table of Contents

Introduction

The purposes of fiction are
to understand our experiences more purposefully than the way
random life shows it and to confront people with reality.

Write a story you care about and believe in.

Ask yourself: "Why does this character's story matter to me?"

To make your voice your own,
ignore the trends,
pursue a story you are passionate about,
and communicate it with the greatest possible impact.

Guided by the foregoing insights of Orson Scott Card and Margaret Lucke, the 5 short short stories in this volume were written in Brampton (Ontario)—which is also the setting of stories 1 to 4. The stories address the following central issues:

1. *How do people strike a balance—or choose—between agape (selfless kindness) and eros (sexual passion)?*

2. *How do people cope when their loved ones shake the foundations of their faith?*

3. *Can the native English speaker's claim to superiority over non-native English speakers prevail in an age of Global Englishes?*

4. *How can a person be a neighbour in an environment of divergent cultures and social locations? (How can an erstwhile visible majority white Canadian cope when she becomes a visible minority white Canadian?)*

5. *How does one become someone? Can a person create their own identity outside their family's shadow? How does one earn honour?*

Synopsis: The Prospect

1. *The central issue: How do people strike a balance—or choose— between agape (selfless kindness) and eros (sexual passion)?*
2. *The premise: An Indian interpreted his failure to be a doctor in Canada as karma for aborting female fetuses when he was a doctor in India. He thought he could atone for his past by teaching non-discrimination to his ESL students and later, by rescuing an Indian lady student from an abusive marriage.*
3. *The protagonist's main goal: Avtar wanted to redeem himself by educating his fellow Indians about non-discrimination as an ESL teacher, guided by Canada's Charter of Rights and Freedoms.*
4. *The central conflict is with a social force—i.e., India's culture of discrimination expressed in misogyny, casteism, and sexual repression. This has roots in the practice of dowry that a bride's family is expected to give to the groom's family.*
5. *The protagonist's constraints: Avtar failed to teach non-discrimination to his students because misogyny is ingrained in their homes. In class, he saw bruised wives and observed casteist behaviours. He failed to rescue Harpreet from her abusive marriage because he eventually developed a relationship with her brother, Kamal.*

6. *Suspense is generated by eliminating the options (see: items 5 & 7). Avtar's students could not behave in a non-discriminatory way because misogyny is rooted in Indian culture. Moreover, his resolved love for women—perhaps for Harpreet—was agape (selfless kindness) and his philia (deep friendship) with Kamal became eros (sexual passion).*

7. *The chain of cause-and-effect (or action-and-consequence):*

   a. *Because Avtar twice failed the qualifying exam to be a doctor in Canada*
      → he believed his failure was karma for aborting female fetuses when he was a doctor in India
      → he wanted to change his karma by helping deconstruct India's culture of discrimination
      → he became an ESL teacher and taught his students the Canadian Charter of Rights and Freedoms

   b. *Because he spent his youth on his career as a medical student and a doctor*
      → he forfeited—or postponed—his chances to engage in a love relationship
      → he longed for, and decided to find, a love relationship in the liberal environment of Canada

   c. *Because Avtar showed concern for the abusive marriage of Harpreet*
      → he became a friend to Harpreet and her brother, Kamal
      → Harpreet began to see Avtar as a prospective second husband

   d. *Because their after-class cafeteria meetings became a habit*
      → Avtar, Harpreet, and Kamal developed philia (deep friendship)

→ *Avtar and Kamal met even when Harpreet was absent "because of family issues"*

→ *Avtar and Kamal's philia developed into eros*

8. *The conflict is resolved—not for the protagonist, but—only for the reader. Avtar failed to redeem himself because Indian misogyny can change only if a critical mass of Indians "act changed." (Behaviour changes precede belief changes.) Moreover, Avtar could not completely rescue Harpreet from her abusive marriage by being her second husband because he developed a love relationship with Kamal.*

The Prospect

We gave the *Kama Sutra* to the world more than 2,000 years ago. Some of our gods are half-male and half-female. Why are we sexually repressed today? Avtar asked himself and threw up his hands in rage as he watched the CBC TV news report: *India's Supreme Court criminalizes gay sex.* Has the world's largest democracy returned to colonial 1860?

Standing 5'9" and 162 pounds, Avtar focused his shaven oval face on the TV report. Half an inch of skin separated his thick dark eyebrows, while a broadening forehead isolated his short wavy hair from his once-handsome features—tapered eyes, prominent nose, aging lips, and jutted chin. He was born in Hoshiarpur in 1972, became a doctor at 28 in 2000, practised for five years, and immigrated to Canada

35 in 2007. He was now 40. He lived in Brampton—a flat landscape that South Asians now called home—some 32 kilometers west of Toronto. He rented an apartment on Hanover Road, a three-minute walk from the Bramalea City Centre. On his first visit to Toronto, he was intrigued by posters that announced that many Punjabi taxi drivers have either an M.D. or a Ph.D. To be a doctor in Canada, he needed to pass the exams of the Medical Council and the Royal College of Physicians and Surgeons. He failed the qualifying exam twice. Some 7,500 foreign doctors who had passed the exam failed to earn a spot in the 236 residency positions. This career path is awfully long and unpromising for me, he concluded then. Is it *karma?* His question transported him back to Punjab where mothers-in-law paid him to abort the female fetuses of their daughters-in-law. I—a murderer? He opened a bottle of cold Molson Canadian beer and sipped.

In anticipation of International Women's Day, the CBC was synthesizing *South Asian Daughters*—a report which included recent events that attracted global attention. *An Indian girl is raped every 22 minutes in a culture of impunity. India Child Development Minister reports 2,000 female fetuses aborted daily. Caste discriminations sting in Hindu temples and Sikh gurdwaras.* Two headlines hit Avtar hard. *Casteism, misogyny, and sexual repression: India's culture of discrimination. 9 out of 10 rape cases unreported; it is futile to turn to uncaring doctors.* Avtar sipped again. He opened another bottle of lager beer. By God, it is *karma!* I was uncaring…a murderer…What can I do to change my *karma?*

Rather than drive a cab, Avtar earned a TESOL certificate at the University of Toronto. Being a bachelor, he had the luxury of time to study. He figured that as a teacher, he could take a small step to deconstruct the Indian culture of discrimination…and change his *karma.* Moreover, he might now find some time to love and be loved—a prospect his past career deprived him of. Within a year, he became an instructor at the LINC (Language Instruction for Newcomers to Canada) Program of the South Asian Centre in Brampton. As a teacher, he taught "Canadian culture"—specifically, the *Canadian Charter of Rights and Freedoms*. His passion for that topic was only briefly a secret. His students heard his voice crack when he spoke about the right to equality. They occasionally saw a tear fall. Among his students in the same class were Harpreet and her brother, Kamal.

"Don't you want to practise medicine in Canada, Avtar?" Harpreet once asked.

"I did, on my first years; but I failed the qualifying exams twice. Canada calls us IMGs or internationally trained medical graduates—a glamorous label for doctors whose skills are suspicious."

"That's quite unfair, don't you think?" Kamal asked.

"I really can't blame the government for its policy. Some immigrants have dubious degrees. I know taxi drivers in Toronto who bought their so-called credentials back home. Recently, the government has been tracking fake marriages, too—men sponsoring women … "

"No wonder the immigration policies are under scrutiny … " Kamal said.

Harpreet Kaur and Kamal Brar immigrated to Canada in 2012. They were born in Jalandhar, in Avtar's state of Punjab. They both had fair skin—fairer than Avtar's. Harpreet, 35, stood 5'5" and 134 pounds. She had a clear oval face, round black soulful eyes, threaded eyebrows, aquiline nose, and half-full lips that displayed a complete set of white teeth when she was clueless about an issue. Her dimpled right cheek appeared balanced by three left-ear diamond studs. She must have needed some thirty minutes to brush her waist-length straigh' black hair. Kamal, 25, stood 5'8" and 158 pounds. His eyes and n' could not disguise his biological link to Harpreet. His widow's peak seemed incongruous in his rectangular face—but not when the five o'clock shadow underscored his narrow mouth. It did so thrice a week. Separated by three-fourths inch of skin, his slim dark eyebrows projected the discipline that his quasi-punk hair style rejected. His broad hands matched the *tabla* he used for his favourite song, *Ishq Sufiyana*.

One Wednesday, Avtar noticed that both Harpreet and Kamal entered the classroom an hour late. Did their gait betray anxiety—or despair? Was it a cry for help? After dismissing the class, Avtar asked Harpreet and Kamal to join him at the school cafeteria.

"Are those bruises on your arm, Harpreet?"

"They are…from my husband, Vijay." Harpreet flushed in anger and embarrassment.

"It's been going on for years, but it worsened soon after we joined your class," volunteered Kamal. "My sister finally mustered some courage to say she's a person and not Vijay's chattel."

"And what do you do, Kamal, when Vijay hurts your sister?"

"What can I do? I stay at their basement rent-free; the door between us is barred from their side. Vijay is our second cousin."

"What do you want to do, Harpreet?"

"I want to leave Vijay, but I have nothing. He sponsored me to come to Canada. My in-laws keep my passport and jewels. I have nowhere to go. Vijay has threatened to deport me back to India…to separate me from our two children. I know my life will not be safe there; I have no means of support. Will you help me…process my divorce?"

"Let me … "

"How I wish my husband were as gentle as you, Avtar. Thank you for taking care of my brother and me…of me."

A long silence followed. At a loss for words, Avtar gently embraced the sister and brother who reciprocated without hesitation. Tears wet their collars.

For months, Avtar, Harpreet, and Kamal exchanged variations of this conversation at the school cafeteria where they had become habitués—often the only ones at 5:30 p.m. Gradually, Harpreet began skipping the class "because of family issues." Avtar and Kamal continued their cafeteria rendezvous and became better acquainted. Their conversations began to shift from Harpreet's situation to their own similarities. Both had abandoned the name "Singh" and their turban within seven months of their arrival in Canada. They both wore neither the *kesh* (long uncut hair), nor the *kangha* (a hair comb), nor the *kaccha* (undergarment shorts). They still wore the *kara* (a bracelet) and kept their *kirpan* (a short sword) at home. Both admired Piscine Molitor Patel in *Life of Pi* and Rajesh Koothrappali in *The Big Bang Theory*. They embraced each other goodbye before parting ways each evening—the way they did when Harpreet was around.

Harpreet's divorce was finalized a week before *Raksha Bandhan,* the festival that celebrated love and duty between siblings. On that day, a sister tied a *rakhi* (sacred thread) on her brother's wrist and fed him. For his part, a brother gave his sister a gift and promised to protect her. On the class day after the festival, Avtar, Harpreet, and Kamal were back at the cafeteria. With a red *bindi* between her eyebrows, and dressed in a daintily seductive *shalwar kameez* on this 26°C mid-August day, Harpreet rather resembled a bride going to her wedding than a divorcée facing an unknown future.

"Kamal and I have been staying with Manjeet since my divorce, Avtar. She has an unfinished basement that shelters us temporarily." Harpreet served *samosas* with mint chutney and piping hot Masala chai.

"I see. What's your prospect, though, Harpreet…your next step?"

7

"I was hoping to marry again…a gentle Punjabi who can love a woman as a woman. Does such a man exist, Avtar? Will you … " Before she could complete her plea, Harpreet noticed the *rakhi* she had tied on Kamal's wrist the day before. She noticed something else too. Kamal and Avtar were wearing each other's *kara*. Silence prevailed. "Oh, I'm sorry … *Namaste,* Avtar."

—End—

Synopsis: The In-law

1. The central issue: How do people cope when their loved ones shake the foundations of their faith?

2. The premise: A 69 year-old mother insisted that Jesus is the Son of God; her 48-year old son, Roco, replied that Jesus was the son of a Palestinian carpenter. The mother struggled with the fact that her son had abandoned their family's traditional Catholicism and yet had matured into a responsible man with clear commitments—perhaps due to the influence of his wife, an academic scholar of religions.

3. The protagonist's main goal: Marta aimed to convince Roco again that happiness can be found only in traditional Catholic piety—the way she convinced him in his youth.

4. The central conflict is with a force within oneself—i.e., by nature, a person searches for plausibility structures (a creed and a code for living) that resonate meaningfully with their experiences.

5. The protagonist's constraints: After immigrating to Canada, Marta gradually became aware that not everyone was a traditional Catholic. Brampton was populated by non-Christians, non-Catholic Christians, and non-believers. It had both a Catholic and a secular school board. Vera, her daughter-in-law who studied

religions academically, taught and wrote about religion things that Marta could not accept. Marta had also become aware of embarrassing aspects of Catholicism—second guesses on beliefs, sex scandals, indiscretions among fellow Catholics such as her husband, etc.

6. Suspense is generated by raising the stakes—i.e., by increasing the power of suffering by showing its causes and effects more (see: items 5 & 7).

7. The chain of cause-and-effect (or action-and-consequence):

   a. Because Marta lived a traditional Catholic worldview all her life
      → she raised Roco in that worldview
      → she assumed that worldview to be the only meaningful worldview for everyone

   b. Because Vera, Marta's daughter-in-law, was an academic scholar of religions
      → she sought to understand religions in defensible human terms (—not in inscrutable catechism terms)
      → she wrote to articulate truth (—not to defend or offend any status quo)

   c. Because Marta emigrated from a traditional Catholic setting to a multi-cultural / multi-religious setting
      → she became exposed to non-Catholic ways of believing and living
      → she articulated the dissonance between what Catholics say and what they do
      → she experienced both the humanity of Vera and the dissonance between their beliefs

8. The conflict is resolved—not for the protagonist, but—only for the reader. Marta failed to convert Roco back to her traditional

worldview. Then she learned that Vera's humanity—and serenity—comes from faith in life, rather than in confessional statements. Vera believed that life is good—it is worth living. When Marta asked, "Do you still believe, Vera?" Vera sidestepped by saying "I'll pick you up next Saturday, Mom." Marta experienced the coherence of Vera's belief in life and how she lived her life—how she cared for Marta, for her own (i.e., Vera's) family, for intellectual honesty, for people at the hospice, etc. Whether or not Marta abandons her traditional worldview is immaterial. After all, she was 69.

The In-law

"WHy didn't you tell me you married an atheist?" Marta pursed her lips and squinted. "Years ago, you introduced her to me as a scholar of religions."

"Vera *isn't* an atheist, Mom; she *is* a scholar of religions." Roco turned off the radio. Toronto's classical station 96.3 was playing Richard Addinsell's *Warsaw Concerto*—which had stirred Marta's passions on several occasions in the past.

Marta, Roco, and Vera immigrated to Canada from the Philippines in 1997. They were then 52, 31, and 26 years old, respectively. Marta, 69, stood 5'6". Her dyed and coiffed hair, wardrobe variety, and fair features served her well at church functions. Roco, 48, stood 5'7". His deep eyes and unambiguous nose often prompted others to do

11

a double take with the question, "Latino?" Vera, 43, stood 5'6". Her countenance and fashion sense were what connoisseurs described as "simple, elegant." Her preference for earth colours seemed to reflect her scholarly pursuits.

"Have you read her essay on Jesus?" Marta asked.

"Of course, I have; we talk about it regularly," Roco said.

"She says that Jesus was the son of a Palestinian carpenter … "

"Jesus *was* the son of a Palestinian carpenter, Mom."

"Jesus *is* the Son of God, Roco! I've taught you that from birth."

Marta, Roco, and Vera come from a country that prided itself as "the only Catholic country in Asia" with its strain of Spanish religion and Anglo-Saxon education. They settled in Brampton, Ontario, the ninth largest city in Canada about 32 kilometers northwest of Toronto. A majority of its half-million population spoke English as their mother tongue; the rest spoke Punjabi, Urdu, Portuguese, Gujarati, Spanish, Hindi, Tamil, Filipino, Italian, and French. Two school boards operated Anglophone public schools—one was Catholic, the other was secular. Half of the population identified with such Christian groups as Catholic, Anglican, United Church, Lutheran, Baptist, Reformed, and Eastern Orthodox. Others were Sikhs, Hindus, Muslims, and those who did not identify with any religion.

"Throughout history, people have viewed Jesus in various ways, Mom," Roco said. "The Orthodox view him as a risen Lord, Protestants view him as a teacher and a healer, Catholics as a man of sorrows … "

" … the Son of God, Roco. What do you mean 'Catholics'? Aren't you a Catholic anymore?"

"Like the rest of humankind, Vera and I search for truth, Mom. But we avoid those who have found it."

"Vera has converted you, hasn't she?"

"My wife doesn't convert anyone, Mom. We discuss many things at breakfast and dinner—including life and death. She's not a preacher. She is a scholar who seeks to understand religions in defensible human terms rather than in inscrutable catechism terms. She neither defends nor offends any religious *status quo;* she writes to articulate truth."

"Don't you go to church anymore?"

"We all need a sacred space, Mom, but it is much more than the church we go to on some days."

Marta snatched an embroidered handkerchief from her home altar, wiped a tear on her left eye, and sniffed. Roco noticed a fourth altar statue—a sandstone *Pieta.* It looked new. To give it prominence, the three statues that Marta had safeguarded for years were relocated on the altar: a mahogany *Jesus Nazareno,* a sycamore *Mater Dolorosa,* and a bronze Jesus on a cedar cross. "I offered you to God when you were born, Roco. I prayed you'd be a priest to redeem your prodigal father … " The ding-dong of Marta's Nokia cellphone interrupted her. "Hello, Vera?" Marta turned on the speaker of her cellphone.

"Hi, Mom. Do you remember how we enjoyed the Brampton Farmers' Market last summer? Guess what? It opens again this weekend. Would you like to go there sometime?" Enthusiasm was not Vera's weakness.

"I'd love to, Vera. Winter and spring have kept me home most of the time. Some summer sun should do me good. Are you sure you'd have the time?"

"Of course, I would, Mom. I teach from Mondays to Thursdays and volunteer at the hospice on Fridays. Weekends are for the most important people in my life."

"You're a gem, Vera. How are my grandsons?"

"Victor and Hector are okay in high school, Mom; they both enjoy math and soccer. Shall I pick you up on Saturday morning? The weather on June 19 is forecast to be a fine 24°C."

"Other church volunteers are meeting at home at 9:00, Vera. We're making an inventory of the rosaries we made in the spring so our parish priest can mail them in the afternoon to Catholics in Nigeria. Can you pick me up at 11:00?"

"I'll do that, Mom. Bye."

While Marta was on the phone, Roco browsed *Toronto Star* news clippings on top of receipts, bills, and prayer sheets on Marta's altar. One read: *Jesus' December 25 birth is not a fact, pope declares.* Centuries late, he thought. The other read: *Alex Malarkey recants his 2010 book "The Boy Who Came Back from Heaven." Tyndale House stops publication.* Who were they kidding? Roco asked himself.

"You married a *sui generis*, Roco," Marta said. "I loved her soon after you introduced her years ago. She emanated a serenity that I rarely sense nowadays. She still does. I don't know why she reminds me of the Old Testament Esther...or is it Judith? But when I read her essays on Jesus...what is left for me to believe?" Marta's brow creases sketched a conflicted—a tormented—soul.

"People love you, Mom; you love them too. You believe that, don't you?"

"And oh, the sex scandals plaguing our churches...We're Catholics, Roco."

"That doesn't mean we should be credulous, Mom. Our own scholars at Ateneo de Manila University describe us as medieval folk Catholics who can be cowed by pulpit preachers who say 'Either believe or leave'...We're a superstitious people."

Brampton's downtown core was abuzz on June 19, the first day of the Brampton Farmer's Market. Arm in arm, Marta and Vera relished the scene of fresh produce, meats, dairy, baked goods, and hand-made arts-and-crafts. As they sauntered Main Street from north to south, they overheard bits and pieces of local news. Apparently the government's agriculture policy was driving farmers out of Ontario. "Very restrictive measures," sighed one farmer. "Ontario's fate is bleak," moaned another. The spicy flavor of grilled chicken *souvlaki* seduced Vera's senses.

"Shall we have chicken *souvlaki* for lunch, Mom?" she asked.

"I love chicken *souvlaki* dipped in homemade *tzaziki* sauce," Marta answered.

"Two chicken *souvlakis*, please," Vera smiled at the robust man minding the grill. "So how's our new government affecting your business, sir?"

"Well, our agriculture coalition voted for this government in June, hoping they would support us. Apparently, we didn't know them well. *By their fruits you will know them…*Your *souvlakis*…ten dollars, please."

"By their fruits you will know them … " echoed Marta. "I appreciate Roco's regular visits especially during winter, Vera. He even brought Victor and Hector with him a couple of times."

"That's our Roco, Mom," Vera said.

"I was actually surprised on his first visits. He seemed different. He was not delinquent as a youth, but was aimless for a while. His present *joie de vivre* makes me curious."

"He talked about that phase in his life, Mom. Perhaps things changed when we both decluttered our routine. Our simple life—with your two grandsons—allows us to focus on what is essential. We share our chores, we take the bus, we shop together for our weekly supplies, and we talk to each other a lot…every day."

"Married life becomes him, I think."

"Curiously, I think it becomes me, too, Mom."

The warm Brampton sun brought Marta back to her past in the Philippines. In 1966, she married Arturo, a former classmate at University of Santo Tomas who was an active member of the Knights of Columbus. Marta fell in love again and again as she watched him in Catholic processions dressed up as a knight. She had heard about the knights' drinking sprees after the processions—but she shrugged them off as an expression of the Filipino *macho* image. Arturo joined two other Catholic initiatives—the *Cursillo* and the *Opus Dei*. I wonder why, Marta now asked herself. In 1976, Marta and Arturo joined the *Christian Family Movement* or CFM, a support group for Catholic couples. Husbands and wives on weekend live-in retreats exchanging life-journeys—spiritual or otherwise—proved to be Arturo's undoing. On more than one occasion, he and someone else's wife simply forgot—or ignored—the sixth commandment.

"How do you do it? You live a serene, untroubled life with Roco and your sons."

"We do have our glitches, Mom; but we survive. It's not magic. I suppose it's faith in life. Life is good; we try to make it better."

"Do you still believe, Vera?"

"I'll pick you up next Saturday, Mom."

—*End*—

Synopsis: The Student

1. *The central issue: Can the native English speaker's claim to superiority over non-native English speakers prevail in an age of Global Englishes?*

2. *The premise: An English teacher who was frustrated teaching academic English to his South Asian students decided to learn how to teach workplace English from his Indian-Canadian colleague—who could also be his future wife...but who suspected him of being crypto-colonial.*

3. *The protagonist's main goal: Brett wanted to prove that his obsession with academic English will be vindicated because he would succeed teaching it to South Asians in Brampton the way he succeeded teaching it to South Asians in Leicester.*

4. *The central conflict is with a social force—i.e., the fact that English—like other languages—has been and is constantly evolving. This social force is symbolized by Kiran, a Canadian of Indian ancestry who speaks a Canadian variety of English.*

5. *The protagonist's constraints: First, Brett's Brampton students persisted in using the South Asian English they learned back home. Brett belatedly realized that what they needed was workplace English (rather than academic English). Second, the English of*

his South Asian colleagues—except Kiran—was not very different from that of his students. Third, the Business English Index identified non-native English speaking countries—with the exception of Australia on the 6th place—as the most proficient countries in business English. India was on the 8th place. Fourth, "non-proper" English was ubiquitous in Brampton.

6. *Suspense is generated by isolating the character (see: items 5 & 7).*

7. *The chain of cause-and-effect (or action-and-consequence):*

    a. *Because Brett succeeded teaching academic English to South Asians in Leicester*
        → *he thought he would also succeed doing so to South Asians in Brampton*

    b. *Because Brett was frustrated teaching academic English to his South Asian students*
        → *he decided to learn to teach workplace English from Kiran*

    c. *Because Brett and Kiran spent classroom and extra-classroom time together*
        → *Brett entertained the prospect of Kiran being his future wife*
        → *Kiran—who was partial to the oppressed of the world—began to suspect Brett's crypto-colonialism*

8. *The conflict is not resolved for the protagonist. Brett's circumstances indicate failure (see: item 5). He could not succeed teaching academic English to his South Asian students who needed workplace English. The reader might wish to resolve the conflict. Could Brett succeed establishing a relationship with Kiran—and ask her to be his wife?*

The Student

L unch break at the South Asian Centre cafeteria was busy. It was Thursday at 12:12 p.m. Kiran sat at a corner table by the French windows that looked out into a parking space. She was about to mix some vinaigrette into her salad when Brett pulled the chair to her right and sat down.

"Am I a terrible teacher, Kiran?" Brett cupped his chin with his right hand. "It's the last week of this term and my students still say the same sentences they did when we started six months ago."

"Well, you can't impose your British accent on them, that's for sure. Your British is only one of the plural English dialects."

"I'm talking about syntax—not accents, Kiran. My students keep saying 'My father *he* works,' or 'I *am* agree,' or 'I am *confusing* by you' or 'One of my *friend* is ... '"

"You're not a terrible teacher, Brett."

" ... or 'I'm going *to* shopping,' or 'I'm too *much* busy,'...I'm not giving up, you know. My family is a line of exemplary English teachers from the colonial period; I'll not betray my birthright. My former students at Leicester were also from the same countries— Bangladesh, India, Nepal, Pakistan, Sri-Lanka. If I succeeded in England, I'll succeed in Canada."

The South Asian Centre in Brampton operated an English Program that employed eight teachers: Kiran, a Canadian whose parents come from India; Brett, an Englishman; and six South Asians who immigrated to Canada past their 40s. Kiran was 27, 5'6", and 154 pounds. She streaked her shoulder-length ebony hair except her bangs. Her trimmed eyebrows framed dark brown eyes that exuded ominous authority. She wore a *koka* (gold pin) on her aquiline nose, gloss on her timid lips, and bangles on both arms. Her unobtrusive make-up highlighted the sincerity of her pretty oval face. Brett was 35, 5'8", and 160 pounds. His groomed blonde hair, blue eyes, upturned nose, angular cheek bones, and freckled face livened up his sunshine-deprived skin. Students have gotten used to his white long-sleeved shirts, plaid vests, pleated trousers, and polished leather shoes.

"I've been meaning to ask you, Brett—why did you leave England?" Kiran asked.

"I taught for ten years at University of Leicester after earning my degrees there. Then university politics began to smother me…While choking, I realized I needed a life…a wife…Last year, an uncle who had lived in Brampton for half a century invited me to try my luck here. I'm trying. What about you? What's your Canadian story?"

"I was born here a year after my parents emigrated from India. Are you okay in Brampton?"

"Brampton and Leicester are similar in some ways—38.4% of the population here is South Asian; it's 29.9% there. I miss my former students. The fast improvement of their syntax convinced me I was a good teacher."

"Students do not learn one thing perfectly at a time, Brett. They learn numerous things imperfectly all at once and understand what they learn through interrelated evolving stages."

With lunch bags in hand, three fellow teachers smiled and walked past them. One asked another, "Do you remember now where did I see you?" The second one said, "I had these flowers in my garden, but I don't know where did they go." The third one said, "This is the activity that we are going to do it."

Overhearing their sentences, Brett thought, *That* is how my students speak. Wow, my colleagues' sentences are not better than those of my students! Was it the buzzing, chiming, and chirping of assorted ringtones in the cafeteria that made Brett plug both ears with his thumbs? "Your class begins in six minutes, Kiran."

On the way to their office, Brett seemed to be counting the floor tiles. He said nothing to Kiran who contrived a cheerful "Ciao!" as she entered her classroom. He merely shrugged.

Are you a failure, Brett? he asked himself. You're obsessed with teaching your students *proper* English, aren't you? You must have been devastated when you heard your fellow teachers' sentences. He felt his pocket, took out an immaculately-pressed white handkerchief, and blew his nose subtly. Why are you teaching your Leicester kind of academic English to Brampton students who need workplace English? Aren't you compensating for your past disappointments with university politics? The South Asian Centre is *not* a university, Brett. It is an immigrant settlement services agency. Kiran teaches only the grammar required by her students' workplaces. Shouldn't you? He quietly blew his nose again and dabbed his eyes. Ah, Kiran…I should spend more time with you to know you better as a teacher…as my future wife …

The next day, Brett sat in Kiran's afternoon class to observe her communicative approach. To reciprocate her accommodation, Brett offered her a cup of coffee at the cafeteria after class. This first day became a second day and the first week became the first month. Kiran basked in the poetic justice of an Indian woman teaching an Englishman how to teach English. Brett relished the company of Kiran—Indian colour, English intellect…inscrutable yet not impossible …

"Do you enjoy grammar lessons, Kiran?" Brett once asked.

"I enjoy teaching the grammar that I recall. Grammar is actually not a part of our regular school language curriculum in Canada. I learned serious grammar when I completed my TESL certificate at the University of Saskatchewan."

"Listening to your students' sentences today, I felt that the communicative approach has its place in the classroom; but so do focused grammar, substitution, rote-learning, and other so-called 'non-communicative' approaches."

"You miss academic English, don't you, Brett?"

"Frankly, I do; but it's more than that. I get amused when I hear you Canadians add a plural noun to the structure 'There is'—as in *'There's six books'*...or when you sprinkle your sentences liberally with the filler 'like'—as in *'There's like six books'*...But when I hear our South Asian colleagues' English sentences, my amusement ends."

"Did you once tell me that you trace your family of English teachers to the colonial period in India?"

"I did—1860 onward."

"Do you think the British rule improved the lives of Indians?" Kiran laid on the coffee table a book she had begun to read a week ago—*Canada's Aboriginals*.

"I certainly do. England's civilizing mission from 1757 to 1947 tamed India's savage practices and eradicated its barbaric beliefs. Don't you agree, Kiran?"

"I don't doubt the British mission of civilization, but I question its cultural imperialism. Education was a strategy for subjugation. Do you think our South Asian colleagues here are intellectually dull and inferior—the way the British regarded my forefathers and foremothers?"

Sensing imminent discomfort, Brett said, "I don't think they're dull and inferior, Kiran. But being English teachers, their sentences ought to be credible."

"Impeccable grammar, Brett?"

"Credible English, Kiran, like yours or Shaun Majumder's of TV's *Just for Laughs*."

Kiran froze momentarily and recalled a recent TV documentary on Thomas Macaulay's *English Education Act of 1835...persons who were Indian in colour, but English in intellect.* Is Brett crypto-colonial? She said, "The Business English Index in California had identified the ten most proficient countries in business English. Do you know that Australia is the only native English speaking country on that list? It ranks sixth. The Philippines ranks first, followed by Norway, Estonia, Serbia, and Slovenia—all non-native English speakers. India ranks eighth. The UK, the US, and Canada are *not* on the list."

"I'd like to read that research. We're just exchanging views here, right? We're not defending ideologies, are we?"

"Views reflect ideologies, Brett. There are still *haves* and *have nots* in Canada—in the world—where conflicting interests are constantly at play. The dynamic is the same between native speakers and non-native speakers."

"English is English, Kiran."

"Not anymore, Brett. English has become Englishes. A native speaker is not more proficient than a non-native speaker who can deal with a Chinese or a Greek accent—specifically with an outsourced call centre in Karachi. You're not crypto-colonial, are you?"

Brett shrugged his shoulders. That was their last conversation on Friday. As Brett walked toward the parking space, four wall posters caught his eyes. *Have a happier holidays.* Who authorized the combination of an indefinite article plus a comparative plus a plural noun? he wondered. *Tim Hortons. Toronto Maple Leafs. Skateboarding and rollerblading is prohibited.* Doesn't Hortons need an apostrophe 's—*Horton's?* When did the word *leafs* supersede the plural form *leaves?* Are *skateboarding and rollerblading* considered a single unit in Canada the way spaghetti and meatballs are?

—*End*—

Synopsis: The Neighbour

1. *The central issue: How can a person be a neighbour in an environment of divergent cultures and social locations? (How can an erstwhile visible majority white Canadian cope when she becomes a visible minority white Canadian?)*
2. *The premise: A welfare-poor Canadian mother struggled with the fact that her middle class immigrant neighbours refused to allow her daughter to use their driveway for her chalk drawings, yet they seemed to care in other ways.*
3. *The protagonist's main desire: Rebecca wanted to return to and relive the good ol' days when neighbours were caring folk rather than uncaring strangers.*
4. *The central conflict is with a social force—i.e., the fact that the complexion of neighbourhoods change. In this neighbourhood, the erstwhile white Canadians have become the minority and are the welfare poor.*
5. *The protagonist's constraints: Unlike Rebecca's family, the neighbours had university degrees and jobs; they valued their privacy and had precious little time to socialize with them. Brampton's sprawling subdivisions kept people segregated as people drove to work, to big-box stores, and then back to their homes. Immigrants*

had become two-thirds of Brampton. White residents dwindled because of retirement, low birth rate, and white flight—i.e., they have left because they were not comfortable being the minority.

6. *Suspense is generated by isolating the character. Rebecca felt left out as a welfare poor Canadian vis-à-vis her middle class immigrant neighbours (see: items 5 & 7). Moreover, hers was a dysfunctional family. George fathered her first two children, Sandra and Chris. Craig fathered Carol. Sandra hates Craig; Chris hates Rebecca, Craig, and Sandra. More than once, Rebecca had called the police on Chris for aggression. Rebecca's attempts to be friendly were mistrusted by her neighbours who had witnessed police officers investigate their domestic disputes on several occasions.*

7. *The chain of cause-and-effect (or action-and-consequence):*

    a. *Because Rebecca and Craig were raised in Ottawa farms*
        → they could do only odd jobs in Brampton; and they had time on their hands

    b. *Because Rohan and Lulu were educated in Holland where they had worked*
        → they kept their middle class jobs when their company moved to Brampton

    c. *Because Rohan and Lulu had Monday-to-Friday jobs*
        → they had little time to socialize with Rebecca and Craig
        → they paid Craig to mow their lawn and shovel their snow

    d. *Because Rohan and Lulu had little time to socialize with their neighbours*
        → they compensated for that "absence" by participating in the local school's fund-raising drive, by welcoming neighbourhood kids on Halloween, and by reciprocating Craig's Christmas gifts

8. *The conflict is resolved—not for the protagonist, but—only for the reader. Rebecca could never relive the good ol' days. She could only dream of it because her neighbourhood had evolved. Cultural issues divided the city. Moreover, Rebecca had her own family issues. As the story ended, paramedics brought out someone on a bed-sheet covered stretcher (Rebecca? Sandra?) while the police was interviewing Chris. Rebecca's daughter, Carol, sobbed and clung to their neighbours—who were no other than Rohan and Lulu.*

The Neighbour

"**W**hat the hell?" Rebecca slammed her front screen door. "Rohan told Carol to wash off her chalk drawings on his driveway and never to draw there again? Our daughter is upset."

Rebecca and Rohan were neighbours. Their driveways were parallel, distinguished only by the darker shade of Rohan's side—a result of regular upkeep.

"I asked Rohan to let tomorrow's rain wash off the drawings," Craig said, "but he wants his driveway clean all the time."

"But we're neighbours! Shouldn't they be neighbourly?"

"For Rohan, that means respecting boundaries, Rebecca. *Good fences make good neighbours,* he said. Tell Carol to draw only on our driveway."

Bramalea Court was a neighbourhood in Brampton—the ninth largest city in Canada about 32 kilometers northwest of Toronto, the capital of Ontario. Some 88% of its residents were recent immigrants. Three homes belonged to white Canadians, two to mixed partners, and twenty-eight to families from South Asia, East Europe, and Latin America.

Rebecca lived at #2 Bramalea Court with her second partner, Craig; and their seven-year old daughter, Carol. Both of Irish descent, Rebecca, 49, and Craig, 59, were born and raised in Ottawa farms. Rebecca moved to Brampton in 1995 with her first partner, George; and their kids—Sandra, 25; and Chris, 22. Craig moved to Brampton in 2001 as a handyman—the circumstance under which he met Rebecca who then was already separated from George. When the neighbour-hood schools were open, Rebecca and Craig worked as crossing guards. Rebecca occasionally cared for a neighbour's child or walked a neighbour's dog. Craig repaired household stuff for neighbours and distributed the *Brampton Guardian* and store flyers twice weekly around the Bramalea Court. Both were otherwise unemployed.

Rohan, 59, and Lulu, 53, lived at #1 Bramalea Court with their two sons—Mark, 25, and Dirk, 22. Jamaican by birth, they had lived in Holland for three decades and immigrated to Canada in 2007 when their company, *De Lage Landen,* set up a Brampton branch. Rohan and Lulu were graduates of Rotterdam School of Management, Erasmus University. They met at their company where Rohan was a commercial finance account coordinator and Lulu was a bilingual contract administrator. They did the same jobs in Brampton.

"I know you chat with Rohan, Craig." Rebecca said.

"He pays me some $12 to mow his lawn twice a month in summer and to shovel his driveway in winter."

"Do you talk to him about us?"

"I'm sure he's seen George on our driveway some weekend. He asked what school Sandra and Chris go to. I said they're not keen on schools."

"He once asked Carol what books she reads in school." Rebecca lit up a stick of cannabis. Its strong scent merged with other evening smells when skunks and raccoons claimed the backyards as their territory. "You think Rohan and Lulu are good folks?"

"They let the kids play on their driveway, don't they?" Craig cleared his throat, took Rebecca's stick, puffed once, and returned it.

" ... but not to mess it up with chalk drawings. They have sons, right?"

"Yeah—university guys. Rohan and Lulu support the schools' fundraising drive—you know, when Carol sells chocolate bars in the fall," Craig added.

"Oh yeah, Lulu welcomes the neighbourhood kids on Halloween. They exchange Christmas gifts with you, don't they? Decent folks?... Hmm...What do you chat about?"

"Small talk...nothing more. Neighbours have seen you cuss out Chris on the street, Rebecca; they've seen police cars parked in our front almost every week last summer. They are not dumb, you know," Craig said.

"Yeah, Chris's pot and drugs are a public secret in Brampton. So they've seen Sandra cuss you out, too?"

"I bet they have." Your daughter hates me; your son hates you, his sister, and me, Craig thought. Watch out, Rebecca. You've called the police on Chris for aggression more than once. We don't know how far he might go.

Rebecca collected her newly-dyed waist-long black hair and clipped it with a floral hair clip one might see at Dollarama. "Do you miss the farms in Ottawa, Craig?"

"Wide trails, maple groves, small cedars, red oak plantations … "

"No neighbours … "

"No neighbours, Rebecca? Folks are cool if they're not too different. Remember our first years here at Bramalea Court?"

"Yeah—neighbours looked out for each other then. Home garden harvests, street hockey games, pajama parties…I miss the summer barbecues of Bruce and Maria. She made her sauce zingy with lemon, pineapple, and some Filipino spices, I think … "

"Neighbourhood watch, driveway shoveling teams, spring clean groups, and garage sales … " Craig added.

"Folks were not too different from each other then, Craig; we were mostly white folks here in Bramalea Court."

"We were, weren't we? Only the Canadian-Filipino and the Canadian-Jamaican families were different then."

"Different, but cool … the good ol' days … " Rebecca reminisced.

"We can't return to the good ol' days, Rebecca. Who's got the time? Only *we* do— the so-called welfare poor of Canada—white Canadians who go to Food Banks. Our neighbours have real jobs, you know.

At the Brampton City Hall the next morning, the council was discussing the city's ten-year development plan. One councilor said, "Our current population is 67% visible minority; 40% of that is South Asian. Do we have a program for that demographic change?" Another asked, "Shouldn't we reassess the bylaw allowing fireworks on *Diwali?* What is our position on large prayer services in residences, parking around places of worship, and basement apartments?" A third one said, "Property values decrease because of packed residential homes. Those extra units result in overcrowded schools, roads, and hospital emergency rooms." The mayor noted, "Isn't it ironic that only one out of our 23 councilors is non-white in a city that is only 33% white?" A fourth councilor observed, "Toronto has its own ethnic enclaves—Black, Chinese, Greek, Italian, Jewish, Portuguese—but they eventually come together. Brampton's case seems to be different. White residents and South Asians are on different pages ... " The council discussions commanded the next issues of the *Toronto Star* and the *Brampton Guardian*.

White Canadians, mixed partners, South Asians, East Europeans, Latin Americans—Craig thought while doing his newspaper rounds. He folded the *Brampton Guardian* and put it in the mailbox of Scott and Donna, the other white Canadian couple at Bramalea Court. Scott, 73, and Donna, 70, lived at #28, where they had raised three children. Originally from Cape Breton, they moved to Brampton in their early 30's, taught at various public schools, and retired.

"How you doin' Craig? Heard about our city council's recent talks on TV?" Scott asked as he caressed his stone garden gnome. He was in his patio with Donna who smiled and waved a hello.

"They might be in today's papers; haven't read them," Craig said.

"Times are different, Craig. The recent immigrants are two-thirds of Brampton; we who welcomed them decades ago are dwindling fast."

"Our folks are retiring and none of us have a lot of kids, Scott."

"It's more than that, I guess. We were then the visible majority, but we're now the visible minority. You okay with that scenario?"

"Cultural issues are dividing our city," Donna volunteered. "Parking on the streets around Hindu temples and Sikh *gurdwaras,* basement apartments that overcrowd our schools and roads ... If we raise these issues in public, we might be called bigots. We don't want that, do we? That's so un-Canadian. We don't want isolated communities—white groups and non-white groups. We're all immigrants, after all."

"Yeah, that sucks," Craig said. "I know folks who've left—uncomfortable or afraid, I can't say. 'White flight,' the papers say."

"Shouldn't our council act on our uncontrolled population? And shouldn't South Asians also adjust their views about being Canadian?" Scott asked.

"Rebecca and I were just talking about the good ol' days. We kinda miss the small town feel of neighbourhoods—of Bramalea Court neighbourhood," Craig said.

"Ah—home garden harvests, summer barbecues, driveway shoveling teams, spring clean groups … " Donna recalled.

Three white-and-blue Brampton Police sedans drove by, followed by an ambulance. They parked in front of #1, #2, and # 3 Bramalea Court.

"Isn't that your home, Craig?" Donna asked.

Craig left his cart of newspapers and rushed home. As he entered their yard, he saw Carol outdoors, sobbing and tightly clinging to Lulu and Rohan. Two police officers were interviewing Chris and three entered the house. Two paramedics brought out a bed-sheet covered stretcher and gently set it down at the back of the ambulance.

Damn … Rebecca? Sandra? Craig wondered.

—*End*—

Synopsis: The Souvenir

1. *The central issue: How does one become someone? Can a person create their own identity outside their family's shadow? How does one earn honour?*
2. *The premise: A 40-year old man deserted his trophy wife and 3 adolescent daughters because her overbearing character choked his search for himself. Although he grew up in a well-off environment, he was never regarded for himself; he was always defined in terms of his parents—and later, in terms of his wife.*
3. *The protagonist's main desire: Ramon wants a little amor proprio—i.e., to be recognized for what he is, rather than only for being the son of his parents or the husband of his wife.*
4. *The central conflict is with a social force—i.e., the Filipino cultural preference for such status symbols as the law profession (with its expectation of affluence), being a mestiza (with its neo-colonial subtext), and having a son (with its macho connotation).*
5. *The protagonist's constraints: Ramon studied law only because his parents—who were lawyers—expected him to. Then he became known as "the law student with notorious parents." He married a trophy wife, but later realized he became known as "the husband*

of the mestiza ... who is a swindler." He had no son; he had 3 daughters—the first of whom was fathered by someone else.

6. *Suspense is generated by raising the stakes—i.e., by increasing the power of suffering by showing its causes and effects more (see: items 5 & 7).*

7. *The chain of cause-and-effect (or action-and-consequence):*

   a. *Because Ramon's parents were notorious lawyers*
       → *Ramon developed a low self-esteem at an early age and failed to become someone in many things*
       → *Ramon studied law, but did not take the bar to become a bonafide lawyer*

   b. *Because Ramon married an overbearing trophy wife*
       → *his already low self-esteem prevented him from speaking out his mind*
       → *he suffered in silence—he couldn't even inquire who his first daughter's father really was*

   c. *Because Dalia was a mestiza who had no college degree*
       → *she used her physical attributes and glib tongue to earn money—by being a scam artist*

8. *The conflict is not resolved for the protagonist. The reader might wish to resolve it. Ramon's circumstances indicate failure. How can he earn the amor proprio he longs for—and which all humans need? He recalled his karate instructor say that the samurai sword symbolized honour. He was also familiar with the manner the World War II Japanese upheld their honour ... when they failed.*

The Souvenir

B aguio was a highly urbanized city in the Philippines built by the Americans in 1903 on uneven hilly terrain in Benguet some 5,000 feet above sea level. With its tropical pine forests, it was well known to tourists for its "eternal spring" weather, flowers, produce, commerce, schools, and history. It showed traces of the American colonial period—compared to parts of the country that had Spanish footprints.

On September 1, 1995, Ramon married Dalia in Baguio. In the afternoon of their wedding day, the city celebrated the 50th anniversary of Japan's surrender to the Allied Forces—which happened in Baguio in 1945. The mayor awarded souvenir *samurai* swords to its prominent citizens—Ramon's parents among them. Before they passed away, they earned the reputations concomitant to their upper middle class professions. Ramon's mother later gave her souvenir to Ramon, who displayed it on the wall above the mantelpiece that supported Dalia's vase of white orchids called *Phalaenopsis Baguio.*

The marriage of Ramon and Dalia was not exceptional. Like countless couples, they have quarreled about a thousand nothings through the years. A month ago, however, Ramon decided he could not take Dalia's unilateral decisions anymore. He left her with their three adolescent daughters—Dana, Jana, and Lana. After being incommunicado for a month, Ramon mustered enough courage to visit their home which—after all—was a conjugal present given by his parents. He stood before the front door that he slammed shut when he left in anger a month ago. Last month's altercation betrayed irreconcilable differences, Ramon thought. He felt less anger than indifference today.

35

He turned his key, entered the living room, and sniffed the aroma of Benguet coffee. Dalia sat there turning the pages of their wedding album on a pinewood table under a ceramic lampstand. A bowl of red strawberries sat on the same table. The scent of pinewood and the sight of strawberries distracted him with the question, How could I desert my home? She looked at him without saying a word. Ramon returned her gaze; then glanced at the *samurai* sword on the wall. He noticed that the orchids on the vase were the pink *Dendrobium anosmum.* No one said a word for one awkward minute. Dalia cleared her throat.

"Why did you marry me sixteen years ago, Ramon?" she asked.

"I … uh … I loved you then. I still …" He expected a different question. "My friends celebrated me like a hero when they saw you were a *mestiza* and when they learned you were pregnant."

"Huh … Do you love our daughters?"

" … then they mocked me when they learned I wasn't Dana's father. They asked me—they didn't stop asking me if I'll ever have a son." Ramon choked momentarily and looked back at the open door to hide a tear. He thought he maintained his dignified stance.

"I'm sorry, Ramon."

"I'm sorry, too. Our marriage was my ticket out of my parents' shadows. I am no one, Dalia. I am either the son of my parents or the husband of the *mestiza.*"

"Your folks loved you, Ramon."

"You think? They loved their jobs and their social circles, Dalia. They never had time for me—a prop they spent for in schools."

"They gifted us this first floor of your house on our wedding day, remember?"

"They wanted to be near their future grandchildren to make up for lost time. But it's too late, Dalia."

"Is it really?"

"I'm a 40-year old bearded loser estranged from a 37-year old *mestiza* who knows and gets what she wants. Not even my kidney issues can disguise my pain. I've tried to be someone in many things—art, *karate*, music, tennis—with nothing to show for any of them. Someone you know is always better."

"You graduated from law school, Ramon."

"You don't get it, do you? I studied law only because my parents were lawyers. Why do you think I haven't done the bar?" Dalia closed the wedding album and sighed. She picked up the bowl of strawberries and offered it to Ramon. Ramon declined; he retrieved the sword from its wall dowels. "I returned just to collect the *samurai* sword on the wall. Cousin Anton wants to buy it. I've been staying at his basement for a month."

"Where do we go from here, Ramon?"

"Search me, Dalia. After sixteen years, we seem to be nowhere. We're both searching for our own selves away from our families' shadows."

"It's ironic, isn't it? My four siblings worked hard at everything—education, careers, families—and they're content with their lives. You were fed with a silver spoon yet you're so needy even in the company of your beer buddies."

Ramon unsheathed the *samurai* sword and recalled his *karate* instructor say it symbolized honour. He remembered World War II stories—how the Japanese defended their honour with that sword. "Why didn't you earn a college degree and get a job like your siblings did, Dalia? When will you have an honest résumé? Neighbours call you 'the glib *mestiza*' and ... 'a scam artist'—did you know?"

"I was the youngest of five—was always compared. I vowed I'd be different, Ramon. There had to be an easier way to success, I imagined. When I got pregnant and you married me, I thought my instinct was right. When you didn't inquire who Dana's father was, I didn't realize what a big blow that was on your self-esteem or whatever was left of it. I wasn't sure then who he was either. I'm sorry again."

"It doesn't matter now, does it?" Ramon sheathed the *samurai* sword. He noticed that the wall showed evidence where the sword had been. He had not dusted the wall for a month, he thought and left.

Ramon hiked for an hour to his cousin's home. Before entering the basement door, he noticed the sun through the trunks of the tall pine trees on the hills a mile away. The sun will set in an hour, he thought. He opened the door and saw Anton seated by his pinewood coffee table with three coffee mugs. Benguet coffee—his two sons must have swung by. Ramon unsheathed the sword.

"It's neither a *kantana* nor a *wakizashi*," Anton said, "yet it looks genuine." He took it from Ramon and inspected its parts. He enjoyed how the sun's rays bounced off its blade. Spots of reflection danced around the ceiling and walls.

"That's a souvenir *samurai* sword, Anton; it can't be genuine," Ramon said. "Is anything genuine anymore? Forty years have gone and I'm still wondering what I'd like to be when I grow up."

"You have a trophy wife and three lovely daughters, Ramon." Anton sheathed the *samurai* and laid it on his coffee table.

"Oh, I do, don't I? I'm sick of society's *haves* and *don't haves*. People don't really care who I am. They see me as a father with no son, as someone with notorious parents, as a husband with a *mestiza* wife—who is a swindler. I'm pathetic, Anton."

"What does Dalia say?" Anton implicitly agreed with his cousin's analysis.

"Dalia has her own issues, Anton; but she's the latest reason I couldn't find myself. I thought our marriage would mark a new chapter for me. I welcomed a similar thought on my parents' funeral.

People would finally see me for what I am. I was so wrong. My *mestiza* wife governs our home with rules of her own. In fairness, she raised our daughters well, but I'm tired of being no one, Anton."

"Let me write you a cheque for the sword, Ramon. Ninety-five dollars, did you say?" Anton fetched his chequebook from his bedroom on the first floor.

Ramon stared at the sunset and thought, Cancel the cheque, Anton. I don't need it anymore. Keep the *samurai* sword as a souvenir from someone who looked for a little *amor propio* ... who wanted simply to walk down the street with his head high but was denied at every turn. No, I won't be deprived of my honour.

The bells of both the Anglican and the Catholic churches announced the 6:00 p.m. *Angelus*. From afar, a dog whined what sounded like a *Requiem*. The fog slowly enshrouded the valley below.

Anton returned to the basement. "Here's your cheque—and thanks, Ramon. Where are you, Ramon?" Against the last rays of the sunset through the open basement door, Anton saw the silhouette of a dog lying still on the grass. Ramon was nowhere. So was the souvenir.

—*End*—

Reading
Comprehension

The Prospect

Instruction A: Match the words on the left column with the meanings on the
right column by writing the correct letters (a to l) on the lines provided.

.... repressed (adj)   a. not likely to be successful

.... intrigued (adj)   b. no risk for punishment

.... unpromising (adj)   c. an event that will probably happen

.... anticipation (n)   d. to do something that has been done to you

.... impunity (n)   e. having feelings that are not allowed to
                            be expressed

.... misogyny (n)   f. to break down

.... to deconstruct (v)   g. expectation that something will happen

.... incongruous (adj)   h. hatred of women

.... to muster (v)   i. someone who regularly goes to a particular place

.... to reciprocate (v)   j. very interested in something strange
                            or mysterious

.... habitué (n)   k. unsuitable or unexpected

.... prospect (n)   l. to get enough confidence or courage to
                            do something

Instructions B: [1] Read sentences 1 to 10 below. [2] If a sentence is false, write an ✘ after that sentence. [3] Re-write each false sentence as a true sentence on the lines provided. [4] Follow model sentence 1.

1. Vijay, Harpreet's husband, was a classmate of Kamal and Harpreet at a LINC Program.✘

2. Avtar became a doctor at 28 years old and immigrated to Canada at 37 years old.

3. Punjabi mothers-in-law paid Avtar to abort the female fetuses of their daughters-in-law.

4. An IMG who passes Canada's qualifying exam could easily get a spot in the residency positions.

5. By teaching the *Canadian Charter of Rights and Freedoms,* Avtar hoped to change his *karma.*

6. Vijay respected his wife, Harpreet, and treated her as a person.

7. Avtar and Kamal wore their *kesh* (uncut hair), *kangha* (hair comb), and *kaccha* (undergarment shorts).

8. Kamal and Avtar were impressed by Piscine Molitor Patel and Rajesh Koothrappali.

9. Avtar, Harpreet, and Kamal became habitués at *Tandoori Flame Restaurant* after class.

10. Harpreet married Avtar, whom she saw as "a gentle Punjabi who can love a woman."

1. *Vijay, Harpreet's husband, was the second cousin of Kamal and Harpreet.*

The In-law

<u>Instruction A</u>: Match the words on the left column with the meanings on the right column by writing the correct letters (a to l) on the lines provided.

.... double take (n)

.... connoisseur (n)

.... defensible (adj)

.... inscrutable (adj)

.... to articulate (v)

.... *sui generis* (n)

.... conflicted (adj)

.... medieval (adj)

.... to cow (v)

.... superstitious (adj)

.... restrictive (adj)

.... *joie de vivre* (n)

a. can be supported by reason

b. to talk (or write) easily and effectively about a difficult topic

c. confused about a choice (especially about beliefs)

d. to look again because you are surprised by what you saw

e. very old fashioned (The Middle Ages = 500-1500 CE)

f. impossible to know

g. one who knows a lot about something (e.g., art, food, music)

h. feeling of general pleasure and excitement

i. believing in luck; or believing that objects cause events to happen

j. one of a kind

k. to frighten someone to make them do something

l. stops people from doing what they want to do

Instructions B: [1] Read sentences 1 to 10 below. [2] If a sentence is false, write an ✖ after that sentence. [3] Re-write each false sentence as a true sentence on the lines provided. [4] Follow model sentence 1.

1. Marta (52), Roco (31), and Vera (26) immigrated to Canada in 1992. ✖
2. The Philippines had strains of Spanish religion (Catholic) and Anglo-Saxon education (American).
3. A Catholic school board and a Sikh school board operated Brampton's Anglophone public schools.
4. Half of Brampton's population was Christian; others were Hindus, Buddhists, Muslims, and secular.
5. Vera was a scholar who sought to understand religions and to articulate truth.
6. Marta wanted Roco to be a priest so he could redeem her grandsons, Victor and Hector.
7. Roco and Vera had two sons who enjoyed math and soccer in elementary school.
8. Vera reminded Marta of either Esther or Ruth—characters from Old Testament stories.
9. Brampton Farmers' Market sold fresh produce, meats, dairy, baked goods, and arts-and-crafts.
10. As a young man, Roco was delinquent in school and completely aimless at work.

1. *Marta (52), Roco (31), and Vera (26) immigrated to Canada in 1997.*

The Student

Instruction A: Match the words on the left column with the meanings on the right column by writing the correct letters (a to l) on the lines provided.

.... syntax (n)　　　　　　　　a. to have a lot of

.... birthright (n)　　　　　　　b. to completely cover, often in an unpleasant way

.... to exude (v)　　　　　　　c. an agreement between persons of
　　　　　　　　　　　　　　　different views

.... unobtrusive (adj)　　　　　d. the arrangement of words to form phrases
　　　　　　　　　　　　　　　or sentences

.... to smother (v)　　　　　　e. faultless; error-free

.... to contrive (v)　　　　　　f. happening very soon

.... accommodation (n)　　　　g. something you believe you have because of
　　　　　　　　　　　　　　　your origin

.... to bask (v)　　　　　　　　h. to do something in spite of difficulty

.... subjugation (n)　　　　　　i. not easily noticed

.... imminent (adj　　　　　　　j. secret; hidden

.... impeccable (adj)　　　　　k. exploitation

.... crypto (adj)　　　　　　　l. to enjoy an opportunity

Instructions B: [1] Read sentences 1 to 10 below. [2] If a sentence is false, write an ✗ after that sentence. [3] Re-write each false sentence as a true sentence on the lines provided. [4] Follow model sentence 1.

1. British English is the only English dialect. ✗
2. On their first and sixth months in school, Brett's students said the same sentences.
3. Brett's students in Leicester and in Brampton come from South Asia and Latin America.
4. Kiran's parents emigrated from India, where Kiran was born and raised.
5. An Indian woman teaching an Englishman how to teach English is indeed poetic justice.
6. Shaun Majumder of TV's *Just for Laughs* spoke the way Brett's students did.
7. The Business English Index ranked Norway as the most proficient country in business English.
8. A non-native English speaker who can deal with a Chinese or a Greek accent is proficient.
9. These words are correct: *Have a happier holidays / Tim Hortons / Toronto Maple Leafs.*
10. This sentence is correct: *Skateboarding and rollerblading are prohibited.*

1. *British English is not the only English dialect.*

....

....

....

....

....

....

....

....

....

....

....

....

....

....

The Neighbour

Instruction A: Match the words on the left column with the meanings on the right column by writing the correct letters (a to l) on the lines provided.

.... upkeep (n)　　　　a. able to speak two languages equally well

.... boundary (n)　　　b. to ask someone to do something

.... bilingual (adj)　　 c. poor people who are given money by
　　　　　　　　　　　　the government

.... cannabis (n)　　　 d. a little old man with a pointed hat (in
　　　　　　　　　　　　children's stories)

.... to call on (v)　　　e. a person who has a one-sided opinion of others

.... aggression (n)　　 f. maintenance

.... welfare poor (n)　 g. angry or threatening behaviour that usually results
　　　　　　　　　　　　in fighting

.... ironic (adj)　　　　h. to become fewer and fewer

.... gnome (n)　　　　 i. the real or imaginary line that makes the edge of
　　　　　　　　　　　　an area

.... to dwindle (v)　　 j. unusual because the opposite of what is
　　　　　　　　　　　　expected happens

.... bigot (n)　　　　　k. separated

.... isolated (adj)　　 l. a drug that is usually smoked; marijuana

Instructions B: [1] Read sentences 1 to 10 below. [2] If a sentence is false, write an ✗ after that sentence. [3] Re-write each false sentence as a true sentence on the lines provided. [4] Follow model sentence 1.

1. Rebecca, Craig, Carol, George, Sandra, and Chris lived at #2 Bramalea Court. ✗

2. Craig and Rebecca's work hours were from 9:00 a.m. to 5:00 p.m.

3. Originally from Jamaica, Rohan and Lulu moved from Holland to Canada in 2007.

4. Rohan and Lulu were employees of *De Lage Landen* in Holland, France, and Canada.

5. Rohan paid Craig the minimum wage to mow his lawn in summer and to shovel his driveway in winter.

6. Sandra loved Craig; Chris loved his mother (Rebecca), his sister (Sandra), and his step father (Craig).

7. In the past, neighbours did things together: garden harvests, street hockey, and summer barbecues.

8. At present, neighbours had a lot of time for each other because they had no real jobs.

9. Brampton's population was 67% visible minority, 50% of which was South Asian.

10. "White flight" refers to the exit of white Canadians out of Brampton because of fear of being isolated.

1. Rebecca, Craig, Carol, Sandra, and Chris lived at #2 Bramalea Court.

The Souvenir

Instruction A: Match the words on the left column with the meanings on the right column by writing the correct letters (a to l) on the lines provided.

.... concomitant (adj)   a. in a situation where others cannot speak to you

.... unilateral (adj)   b. a short noisy argument

.... incommunicado

   (adv)   c. happening as a result of something

.... altercation (n)   d. to say "no" politely when someone offers
     you something

.... irreconcilable

   (adj)   e. (action or decision) taken by only one person

.... prop (n)   f. to put a sword into its cover

.... to decline (v)   g. impossible to harmonize, to make compatible, or
     to settle

.... to retrieve (v)   h. a woman of mixed race—e.g., Spaniard
     and native

.... *samurai* (n)   i. someone who helps another to feel popular,
     strong, etc.

.... to sheathe (v)   j. to cover or surround

.... *mestiza* (n)   k. to get back

.... to enshroud (v)   l. a member of a powerful Japanese military class in
     the past

Instructions B: [1] Read sentences 1 to 10 below. [2] If a sentence is false, write an × after that sentence. [3] Re-write each false sentence as a true sentence on the lines provided. [4] Follow model sentence 1.

1. Baguio had Spanish traces—compared to other cities that had American traces. ×
2. World War II in the Pacific ended when Japan surrendered in Manila in 1945.
3. *Phalaenopsis Baguio* and *Dendrobium anosmum* are two kinds of roses.
4. Dalia had three daughters—Dana, Jana, and Lana; Ramon had two—Jana and Lana.
5. Ramon's parents received souvenir *samurai* swords on November 1, 1995.
6. Anton bought Ramon's *samurai* sword—which was either a *kantana* or a *wakizashi*.
7. Neighbours did not call Dalia "the glib *mestiza*" and "a scam artist."
8. Baguio was well known to tourists for pinewood, strawberries, Benguet coffee, and orchids.
9. Dalia had four siblings who were successful in their education, careers, and families.
10. During World War II, the Japanese used the *origami* to defend their honour.

1. *Baguio had American traces—compared to other cities that had Spanish traces.*

....

....

....

....

....

....

....

....

....

....

....

....

....

....

....

....